Midnight's Children
Salman Rushdie

This extract first published in the UK in 2003 exclusively for
WHSmith Limited, Greenbridge Road, Swindon SN3 3LD
www.WHSmith.co.uk

Random House, 20 Vauxhall Bridge Road, London, SW1V 2SA

To celebrate the BBC's *The Big Read*

Midnight's Children was first published in the
United Kingdom in 1981 by Jonathan Cape
Published by Vintage in 1995

ISBN 0 0994 6677 5

Typeset by Palimpsest Book Production Limited,
Polmont, Stirlingshire

Printed in Great Britain by Cox & Wyman, Reading

Midnight's Children

One Kashmiri morning in the early spring of 1915, my grandfather Aadam Aziz hit his nose against a frost-hardened tussock of earth while attempting to pray. Three drops of blood plopped out of his left nostril, hardened instantly in the brittle air and lay before his eyes on the prayer-mat, transformed into rubies. Lurching back until he knelt with his head once more upright, he found that the tears which had sprung to his eyes had solidified, too; and at that moment, as he brushed diamonds contemptuously from his lashes, he resolved never again to kiss earth for any god or man. This decision, however, made a hole in him, a vacancy in a vital inner chamber, leaving him vulnerable to women and history. Unaware of this at first, despite his recently completed medical training, he stood up, rolled the prayer-mat into a thick cheroot, and holding it under his right arm surveyed the valley through clear, diamond-free eyes.

The world was new again. After a winter's gestation in its eggshell of ice, the valley had beaked its way out into the open, moist and yellow. The new grass bided its time underground; the mountains were retreating to their hill-stations for the warm season. (In the winter, when the valley shrank under the ice, the mountains closed in and snarled like angry jaws around the city on the lake.)

In those days the radio mast had not been built and the temple of Sankara Acharya, a little black blister on a khaki hill, still dominated the streeets and lake of Srinagar. In those days there was no army camp at the lakeside, no endless snakes of camouflaged trucks and jeeps clogged the narrow mountain roads, no soldiers hid behind the crests of the mountains past Baramulla and Gulmarg. In those days travellers were not shot as spies if they took photographs of bridges, and apart from the Englishmen's houseboats on the lake, the valley had hardly changed since the Mughal Empire, for all its springtime renewals; but my grandfather's eyes – which were, like the rest of him, twenty-five years old – saw things differently . . . and his nose had started to itch.

To reveal the secret of my grandfather's altered vision: he had spent five years, five springs, away from home. (The tussock of earth, crucial though its presence was as it crouched under a chance wrinkle of the prayer-mat, was at bottom no more than a catalyst.) Now, returning, he saw through travelled eyes. Instead of the beauty of the tiny valley circled by giant teeth, he noticed the narrowness, the proximity of the horizon; and felt sad, to be at home and feel so utterly enclosed. He also felt – inexplicably – as though the old place resented his educated, stethoscoped return. Beneath the winter ice, it had been coldly neutral, but now there was no doubt; the years in Germany had returned him to a hostile environment. Many years later, when the hole inside him had been clogged up with hate, and he came to sacrifice himself at the shrine of the black stone god in the temple on the hill, he would try and recall his childhood springs in Paradise, the way it was before travel and tussocks and army tanks messed everything up.

On the morning when the valley, gloved in a prayer-mat, punched him on the nose, he had been trying, absurdly, to pretend that nothing had changed. So he had risen in the bitter cold of four-fifteen, washed himself in the prescribed fashion, dressed and put on his father's astrakhan cap; after which he had carried the rolled cheroot of the prayer-mat into the small lakeside garden in front of their old dark house and unrolled it over the waiting tussock. The ground felt deceptively soft under his feet and made him simultaneously uncertain and unwary. 'In the Name of God, the Compassionate, the Merciful . . .' – the exordium, spoken with hands joined before him like a book, comforted a part of him, made another, larger part feel uneasy – '. . . Praise be to Allah, Lord of the Creation . . .' – but now Heidelberg invaded his head; here was Ingrid, briefly his Ingrid, her face scorning him for this Mecca-turned parroting; here, their friends Oskar and Ilse Lubin the anarchists, mocking his prayer with their anti-ideologies – '. . . The Compassionate, the Merciful, King of the Last Judgment! . . .' – Heidelberg, in which, along with medicine and politics, he learned that India – like radium – had been 'discovered' by the Europeans; even Oskar was filled with admiration for Vasco da Gama, and this was what finally separated Aadam Aziz from his friends, this belief of theirs that he was somehow the invention of their ancestors – '. . . You alone we worship, and to You alone we pray for help . . .' – so here he was, despite their presence in his head, attempting to re-unite himself with an earlier self which ignored their influence but knew everything it ought to have known, about submission for example, about what he was doing now, as his hands, guided by old memories, fluttered upwards, thumbs pressed to ears, fingers spread, as he sank to his knees – '. . . Guide us to the straight path, The path of those whom You have favoured . . .' But it was no good, he was caught in a strange middle ground, trapped between belief and disbelief, and this was only a charade after all – '. . . Not of those who have incurred Your wrath, Nor of those who have gone astray.' My grandfather bent his forehead towards the earth. Forward he bent, and the earth, prayer-mat-covered, curved up towards him. And now it was the tussock's time. At one and the same time a rebuke from Ilse-Oskar-Ingrid-Heidelberg as well as valley-and-God, it smote him upon the point of the nose. Three drops fell. There were rubies and diamonds. And my grandfather, lurching upright, made a resolve. Stood. Rolled cheroot. Stared across the lake. And was knocked forever into that middle place, unable to worship a God in whose existence he could not wholly disbelieve. Permanent alteration: a hole.

The young, newly-qualified Doctor Aadam Aziz stood facing the springtime lake, sniffing the whiffs of change; while his back (which was extremely straight) was turned upon yet more changes. His father had had a stroke in his absence abroad, and his mother had kept it a secret. His mother's voice, whispering stoically: '. . . *Because your studies were too important, son.*' This mother, who had spent her life housebound, in purdah, had suddenly found enormous strength and gone out to run the small gemstone business (turquoises, rubies, diamonds) which had put Aadam through medical college, with the help of a scholarship; so he returned to find the seemingly immutable order of his family turned upside down, his mother going out to work while his father sat hidden behind the veil which the stroke had dropped over his brain ... in a wooden chair, in a darkened room, he sat and made bird-noises. Thirty different species of birds visited him and sat on the sill outside his shuttered window conversing about this and that. He seemed happy enough.

(. . . And already I can see the repetitions beginning; because didn't my grandmother also find enormous ... and the stroke, too, was not the only ... and the Brass Monkey had her birds ... the curse begins already, and we haven't even got to the noses yet!)

The lake was no longer frozen over. The thaw had come rapidly, as usual; many of the small boats, the shikaras, had been caught napping, which was also normal. But while these sluggards slept on, on dry land, snoring peacefully beside their owners, the oldest boat was up at the crack as old folk often are, and was therefore the first craft to move across the unfrozen lake. Tai's shikara ... this, too, was customary.

Watch how the old boatman, Tai, makes good time through the misty water, standing stooped over at the back of his craft! How his oar, a wooden heart on a yellow stick, drives jerkily through the weeds! In these parts he's considered very odd because he rows standing up ... among other reasons. Tai, bringing an urgent summons to Doctor Aziz, is about to set history in motion ... while Aadam, looking down into the water, recalls what Tai taught him years ago: 'The ice is always waiting, Aadam baba, just under the water's skin.' Aadam's eyes are a clear blue, the astonishing blue of mountain sky, which has a habit of dripping into the pupils of Kashmiri men; they have not forgotten how to look. They see – there! like the skeleton of a ghost, just beneath the surface of Lake Dal! – the delicate tracery, the intricate crisscross of colourless lines, the cold waiting veins of the future. His German years, which have blurred so much else, haven't deprived him of the gift of seeing. Tai's gift. He looks up, sees the approaching V of Tai's boat, waves a greeting. Tai's arm rises – but this is a command. 'Wait!' My grandfather waits; and during this hiatus, as he experiences the last peace of his life, a muddy, ominous sort of peace, I had better get round to describing him.

Keeping out of my voice the natural envy of the

ugly man for the strikingly impressive, I record that Doctor Aziz was a tall man. Pressed flat against a wall of his family home, he measured twenty-five bricks (a brick for each year of his life), or just over six foot two. A strong man also. His beard was thick and red – and annoyed his mother, who said only Hajis, men who had made the pilgrimage to Mecca, should grow red beards. His hair, however, was rather darker. His sky-eyes you know about. Ingrid had said, 'They went mad with the colours when they made your face.' But the central feature of my grandfather's anatomy was neither colour nor height, neither strength of arm nor straightness of back. There it was, reflected in the water, undulating like a mad plantain in the centre of his face ... Aadam Aziz, waiting for Tai, watches his rippling nose. It would have dominated less dramatic faces than his easily; even on him, it is what one sees first and remembers longest. 'A cyranose,' Ilse Lubin said, and Oskar added, 'A proboscissimus.' Ingrid announced, 'You could cross a river on that nose.' (Its bridge was wide.)

My grandfather's nose: nostrils flaring, curvaceous as dancers. Between them swells the nose's triumphal arch, first up and out, then down and under, sweeping in to his upper lip with a superb and at present red-tipped flick. An easy nose to hit a tussock with. I wish to place on record my gratitude to this mighty organ – if not for it, who would ever have believed me to be truly my mother's son, my grandfather's grandson? – this colossal apparatus which was to be my birthright, too. Doctor Aziz's nose – comparable only to the trunk of the elephant-headed god Ganesh – established incontrovertibly his right to be a patriarch. It was Tai who taught him that, too. When young Aadam was barely past puberty the dilapidated boatman said, 'That's a nose to start a family on, my princeling. There'd be no mistaking whose brood they were. Mughal Emperors would have given their right hands for noses like that one. There are dynasties waiting inside it,' – and here Tai lapsed into coarseness – 'like snot.'

On Aadam Aziz, the nose assumed a patriarchal aspect. On my mother, it looked noble and a little long-suffering; on my aunt Emerald, snobbish; on my aunt Alia, intellectual; on my uncle Hanif it was the organ of an unsuccessful genius; my uncle Mustapha made it a second-rater's sniffer; the Brass Monkey escaped it completely; but on me – on me, it was something else again. But I mustn't reveal all my secrets at once.

(Tai is getting nearer. He, who revealed the power of the nose, and who is now bringing my grandfather the message which will catapult him into his future, is stroking his shikara through the early morning lake . . .)

Nobody could remember when Tai had been young. He had been plying this same boat, standing in the same hunched position, across the Dal and Nageen Lakes . . . forever. As far as anyone knew. He lived somewhere in the insanitary bowels of the old wooden-house quarter and his wife grew lotus roots and other curious vegetables on one of the many 'floating gardens' lilting on the surface of the spring and summer water. Tai himself cheerily admitted he had no idea of his age. Neither did his wife – he was, she said, already leathery when they married. His face was a sculpture of wind on water: ripples made of hide. He had two golden teeth and no others. In the town, he had few friends. Few boatmen or traders invited him to share a hookah when he floated past the shikara moorings or one of the lakes' many ramshackle, waterside provision-stores and tea-shops.

The general opinion of Tai had been voiced long ago by Aadam Aziz's father the gemstone merchant: 'His brain fell out with his teeth.' (But now old Aziz sahib sat lost in bird tweets while Tai simply, grandly, continued.) It was an impression the boatman fostered by his chatter, which was fantastic, grandiloquent and ceaseless, and as often as not addressed only to himself. Sound carries over water, and the lake people giggled at his monologues; but with undertones of awe, and even fear. Awe, because the old halfwit knew the lakes and hills better than any of his detractors; fear, because of his claim to an antiquity so immense it defied numbering, and moreover hung so lightly round his chicken's neck that it hadn't prevented him from winning a highly desirable wife and fathering four sons upon her . . . and a few more, the story went, on other lakeside wives. The young bucks at the shikara moorings were convinced he had a pile of money hidden away somewhere – a hoard, perhaps, of priceless golden teeth, rattling in a sack like walnuts. Years later, when Uncle Puffs tried to sell me his daughter by offering to have her teeth drawn and replaced in gold, I thought of Tai's forgotten treasure . . . and, as a child, Aadam Aziz had loved him.

He made his living as a simple ferryman, despite all the rumours of wealth, taking hay and goats and vegetables and wood across the lakes for cash; people, too. When he was running his taxi-service he erected a pavilion in the centre of the shikara, a gay affair of flowered-patterned curtains and canopy, with cushions to match; and deodorised his boat with incense. The sight of Tai's shikara

approaching, curtains flying, had always been for
Doctor Aziz one of the defining images of the
coming of spring. Soon the English sahibs would
arrive and Tai would ferry them to the Shalimar
Gardens and the King's Spring, chattering and
pointy and stooped. He was the living antithesis of
Oskar-Ilse-Ingrid's belief in the inevitability of
change . . . a quirky, enduring familiar spirit of the
valley. A watery Caliban, rather too fond of cheap
Kashmiri brandy.

Memory of my blue bedroom wall: on which,
next to the P.M.'s letter, the Boy Raleigh hung for
many years, gazing rapturously at an old fisherman
in what looked like a red dhoti, who sat on – what?
– driftwood? – and pointed out to sea as he told his
fishy tales . . . and the Boy Aadam, my grandfather-
to-be, fell in love with the boatman Tai precisely
because of the endless verbiage which made others
think him cracked. It was magical talk, words
pouring from him like fools' money, past his two
gold teeth, laced with hiccups and brandy, soaring
up to the most remote Himalayas of the past, then
swooping shrewdly on some present detail, Aadam's
nose for instance, to vivisect its meaning like a
mouse. This friendship had plunged Aadam into
hot water with great regularity. (Boiling water.
Literally. While his mother said, 'We'll kill that

boatman's bugs if it kills you.') But still the old solil-
oquist would dawdle in his boat at the garden's lakeside toes and Aziz would sit at his feet until voices
summoned him indoors to be lectured on Tai's
filthiness and warned about the pillaging armies of
germs his mother envisaged leaping from that
hospitably ancient body on to her son's starched
white loose-pajamas. But always Aadam returned to
the water's edge to scan the mists for the ragged
reprobate's hunched-up frame steering its magical
boat through the enchanted waters of the morning.

'But how old are you really, Taiji?' (Doctor Aziz,
adult, redbearded, slanting towards the future,
remembers the day he asked the unaskable question.) For an instant, silence, noisier than a water-
fall. The monologue, interrupted. Slap of oar in
water. He was riding in the shikara with Tai, squat-
ting amongst goats, on a pile of straw, in full knowledge of the stick and bathtub waiting for him at
home. He had come for stories – and with one question had silenced the storyteller.

'No, tell, Taiji, how old, *truly*?' And now a brandy
bottle, materialising from nowhere: cheap liquor
from the folds of the great warm chugha-coat. Then
a shudder, a belch, a glare. Glint of gold. And – at
last! – speech. 'How old? You ask how old, you little
wet-head, you nosey ...' Tai, forecasting the

fisherman on my wall, pointed at the mountains. 'So old, nakkoo!' Aadam, the nakkoo, the nosey one, followed his pointing finger. 'I have watched the mountains being born; I have seen Emperors die. Listen. Listen, nakkoo . . .' – the brandy bottle again, followed by brandy-voice, and words more intoxicating than booze – '. . . I saw that Isa, that Christ, when he came to Kashmir. Smile, smile, it is your history I am keeping in my head. Once it was set down in old lost books. Once I knew where there was a grave with pierced feet carved on the tombstone, which bled once a year. Even my memory is going now; but I know, although I can't read.' Illiteracy, dismissed with a flourish; literature crumbled beneath the rage of his sweeping hand. Which sweeps again to chugha-pocket, to brandy bottle, to lips chapped with cold. Tai always had woman's lips. 'Nakkoo, listen, listen. I have seen plenty. Yara, you should've seen that Isa when he came, beard down to his balls, bald as an egg on his head. He was old and fagged-out but he knew his manners. "You first, Taiji," he'd say, and "Please to sit"; always a respectful tongue, he never called me crackpot, never called me *tu* either. Always *aap*. Polite, see? And what an appetite! Such a hunger, I would catch my ears in fright. Saint or devil, I swear he could eat a whole kid in one go. And so what? I told him, eat, fill your hole, a man comes to Kashmir to enjoy life, or to end it, or both. His work was finished. He just came up here to live it up a little.' Mesmerized by this brandied portrait of a bald, gluttonous Christ, Aziz listened, later repeating every word to the consternation of his parents, who dealt in stones and had no time for 'gas'.

'Oh, you don't believe?' – licking his sore lips with a grin, knowing it to be the reverse of the truth; 'Your attention is wandering?' – again, he knew how furiously Aziz was hanging on his words. 'Maybe the straw is pricking your behind, hey? Oh, I'm so sorry, babaji, not to provide for you silk cushions with gold brocade-work – cushions such as the Emperor Jehangir sat upon! You think of the Emperor Jehangir as a gardener only, no doubt,' Tai accused my grandfather, 'because he built Shalimar. Stupid! What do you know? His name meant Encompasser of the Earth. Is that a gardener's name? God knows what they teach you boys these days. Whereas I' . . . puffing up a little here . . . 'I knew his precise weight, to the tola! Ask me how many maunds, how many seers! When he was happy he got heavier and in Kashmir he was heaviest of all. I used to carry his litter . . . no, no, look, you don't believe again, that big cucumber in your face is waggling like the little one in your pajamas! So, come on, come on, ask me questions! Give examination! Ask how many times the leather thongs wound round the handles of the litter – the answer is thirty-one. Ask me what was the Emperor's dying word – I tell you it was "Kashmir". He had bad breath and a good heart. Who do you think I am? Some common ignorant lying pie-dog? Go, get out of the boat now, your nose makes it too heavy to row; also your father is waiting to beat my gas out of you, and your mother to boil off your skin.'

In the brandy bottle of the boatman Tai I see, foretold, my own father's possession by djinns ... and there will be another bald foreigner ... and Tai's gas prophesies another kind, which was the consolation of my grandmother's old age, and taught her stories, too ... and pie-dogs aren't far away ... Enough. I'm frightening myself.

Despite beating and boiling, Aadam Aziz floated with Tai in his shikara, again and again, amid goats hay flowers furniture lotus-roots, though never with the English sahibs, and heard again and again the miraculous answers to that single terrifying question: 'But Taiji, how old are you, *honestly*?'

From Tai, Aadam learned the secrets of the lake – where you could swim without being pulled down by weeds; the eleven varieties of water-snake; where the frogs spawned; how to cook a lotus-root; and where the three English women had drowned a few years back. 'There is a tribe of feringhee women who come to this water to drown,' Tai said. 'Sometimes they know it, sometimes they don't, but I know the minute I smell them. They hide under the water from God knows what or who – but they can't hide from me, baba!' Tai's laugh, emerging to infect Aadam – a huge, booming laugh that seemed macabre when it crashed out of that old, withered body, but which was so natural in my giant grandfather that nobody knew, in later times, that it wasn't really his (my uncle Hanif inherited this laugh; so until he died, a piece of Tai lived in Bombay). And, also from Tai, my grandfather heard about noses.

Tai tapped his left nostril. 'You know what this is nakkoo? It's the place where the outside world meets the world inside you. If they don't get on, you feel it here. Then you rub your nose with embarrassment to make the itch go away. A nose like that, little idiot, is a great gift. I say: trust it. When it warns you, look out or you'll be finished. Follow your nose and you'll go far.' He cleared his throat; his eyes rolled away into the mountains of the past. Aziz settled back on the straw. 'I knew one officer once – in the army of that Iskandar the Great. Never mind his name. He had a vegetable just like yours hanging between his eyes. When the army halted near Gandhara, he fell in love with some local floozy. At once his nose itched like crazy. He scratched it, but that was useless. He inhaled vapours from crushed boiled eucalyptus leaves. Still no good, baba! The itching sent him wild; but the damn fool dug in his heels and stayed with his little witch when the army went home. He became – what? – a stupid thing, neither this nor that, a half-and-halfer with a nagging wife and an itch in the nose, and in the end he pushed his sword into his stomach. What do you think of that?'

... Doctor Aziz in 1915, whom rubies and diamonds have turned into a half-and-halfer, remembers this story as Tai enters hailing distance. His nose is itching still. He scratches, shrugs, tosses his head; and then Tai shouts.

'Ohé! Doctor Sahib! Ghani the landowner's daughter is sick.'

The message, delivered curtly, shouted unceremoniously across the surface of the lake although boatman and pupil have not met for half a decade, mouthed by woman's lips that are not smiling in long-time-no-see greeting, sends time into a speeding, whirligig, blurry fluster of excitement ...

... 'Just think, son,' Aadam's mother is saying as she sips fresh lime water, reclining on a takht in an attitude of resigned exhaustion, 'how life does turn out. For so many years even my ankles were a secret, and now I must be stared at by strange persons who are not even family members.'

. . . While Ghani the landowner stands beneath a large oil painting of Diana the Huntress, framed in squiggly gold. He wears thick dark glasses and his famous poisonous smile, and discusses art. 'I purchased it from an Englishman down on his luck, Doctor Sahib. Five hundred rupees only – and I did not trouble to beat him down. What are five hundred chips? You see, I am a lover of culture.'

. . . 'See, my son,' Aadam's mother is saying as he begins to examine her, 'what a mother will not do for her child. Look how I suffer. You are a doctor . . . feel these rashes, these blotchy bits, understand that my head aches morning noon and night. Refill my glass, child.'

. . . But the young Doctor has entered the throes of a most unhippocratic excitement at the boatman's cry, and shouts, 'I'm coming just now! Just let me bring my things!' The shikara's prow touches the garden's hem. Aadam is rushing indoors, prayer-mat rolled like cheroot under one arm, blue eyes blinking in the sudden interior gloom; he has placed the cheroot on a high shelf on top of stacked copies of *Vorwärts* and Lenin's *What Is To Be Done?* and other pamphlets, dusty echoes of his half-faded German life; he is pulling out, from under his bed, a second-hand leather case which his mother called his 'doctori-attaché', and as he swings it and himself upwards and runs from the room, the word HEIDEL-BERG is briefly visible, burned into the leather on the bottom of the bag. A landowner's daughter is good news indeed to a doctor with a career to make, even if she is ill. No: *because* she is ill.

. . . While I sit like an empty pickle jar in a pool of Anglepoised light, visited by this vision of my grandfather sixty-three years ago, which demands to be recorded, filling my nostrils with the acrid stench of his mother's embarrassment which has brought her out in boils, with the vinegary force of Aadam Aziz's determination to establish a practice so successful that she'll never have to return to the gemstone-shop, with the blind mustiness of a big shadowy house in which the young Doctor stands, ill-at-ease, before a painting of a plain girl with lively eyes and a stag transfixed behind her on the horizon, speared by a dart from her bow. Most of what matters in our lives takes place in our absence: but I seem to have found from somewhere the trick of filling in the gaps in my knowledge, so that every-thing is in my head, down to the last detail, such as the way the mist seemed to slant across the early morning air ... everything, and not just the few clues one stumbles across, for instance by opening an old tin trunk which should have remained cobwebby and closed.

... Aadam refills his mother's glass and continues, worriedly, to examine her. 'Put some cream on these rashes and blotches, Amma. For the headache, there are pills. The boils must be lanced. But maybe if you wore purdah when you sat in the store ... so that no disrespectful eyes could ... such complaints often begin in the mind ...'

... Slap of oar in water. Plop of spittle in lake. Tai clears his throat and mutters angrily, 'A fine business. A wet-head nakkoo child goes away before he's learned one damn thing and he comes back a big doctor sahib with a big bag full of foreign machines, and he's still as silly as an owl. I swear: a too bad business.'

... Doctor Aziz is shifting uneasily, from foot to foot, under the influence of the landowner's smile, in whose presence it is not possible to feel relaxed; and is waiting for some tic of reaction to his own extraordinary appearance. He has grown accustomed to these involuntary twitches of surprise at his size, his face of many colours, his nose ... but Ghani makes no sign, and the young Doctor resolves, in return, not to let his uneasiness show. He stops shifting his weight. They face each other, each suppressing (or so it seems) his view of the other, establishing the basis of their future relationship. And now Ghani alters, changing from an art-lover to tough-guy. 'This is a big chancé for you, young man,' he says. Aziz's eyes have strayed to Diana. Wide expanses of her blemished pink skin are visible.

. . . His mother is moaning, shaking her head. 'No, what do you know, child, you have become a big-shot doctor but the gemstone business is different. Who would buy a turquoise from a woman hidden inside a black hood? It is a question of establishing trust. So they must look at me; and I must get pains and boils. Go, go, don't worry your head about your poor mother.'

. . . 'Big shot,' Tai is spitting into the lake, 'big bag, big shot. Pah! We haven't got enough bags at home that you must bring back that thing made of a pig's skin that makes one unclean just by looking at it? And inside, God knows what all.' Doctor Aziz, seated amongst flowery curtains and the smell of incense, has his thoughts wrenched away from the patient waiting across the lake. Tai's bitter monologue breaks into his consciousness, creating a sense of dull shock, a smell like a casualty ward over-

powering the incense ... the old man is clearly
furious about something, possessed by an incom-
prehensible rage that appears to be directed at his
erstwhile acolyte, or, more precisely and oddly, at
his bag. Doctor Aziz attempts to make small talk
... 'Your wife is well? Do they still talk about your
bag of golden teeth?' ... tries to remake an old
friendship; but Tai is in full flight now, a stream of
invective pouring out of him. The Heidelberg bag
quakes under the torrent of abuse. 'Sistersleeping
pigskin bag from Abroad full of foreigners' tricks.
Big-shot bag. Now if a man breaks an arm that bag
will not let the bone-setter bind it in leaves. Now a
man must let his wife lie beside that bag and watch
knives come and cut her open. A fine business, what
these foreigners put in our young men's heads. I
swear: it is a too-bad thing. That bag should fry in
Hell with the testicles of the ungodly.'

... Ghani the landowner snaps his braces with
his thumbs. 'A big chance, yes indeed. They are
saying good things about you in town. Good medical
training. Good ... good enough ... family. And now
our own lady doctor is sick so you get your oppor-
tunity. That woman, always sick these days, too old,
I am thinking, and not up in the latest develop-
ments also, what-what? I say: physician heal thyself.
And I tell you this: I am wholly objective in my

business relations. Feelings, love, I keep for my family only. If a person is not doing a first-class job for me, out she goes! You understand me? So: my daughter Naseem is not well. You will treat her excellently. Remember I have friends; and ill-health strikes high and low alike.'

... 'Do you still pickle water-snakes in brandy to give you virility, Taiji? Do you still like to eat lotus-root without any spices?' Hesitant questions, brushed aside by the torrent of Tai's fury. Doctor Aziz begins to diagnose. To the ferryman, the bag represents Abroad; it is the alien thing, the invader, progress. And yes, it has indeed taken possession of the young Doctor's mind; and yes, it contains knives, and cures for cholera and malaria and smallpox; and yes, it sits between doctor and boatman, and has made them antagonists. Doctor Aziz begins to fight, against sadness, and against Tai's anger, which is beginning to infect him, to become his own, which erupts only rarely, but comes, when it does come, unheralded in a roar from his deepest places, laying waste everything in sight; and then vanishes, leaving him wondering why everyone is so upset ... They are approaching Ghani's house. A bearer awaits the shikara, standing with clasped hands on a little wooden jetty. Aziz fixes his mind on the job in hand.

... 'Has your usual doctor agreed to my visit,

Ghani Sahib?' ... Again, a hesitant question is brushed lightly aside. The landowner says, 'Oh, she will agree. Now follow me, please.'

... The bearer is waiting on the jetty. Holding the shikara steady as Aadam Aziz climbs out, bag in hand. And now, at last, Tai speaks directly to my grandfather. Scorn in his face, Tai asks, 'Tell me this, Doctor Sahib: have you got in that bag made of dead pigs one of those machines that foreign doctors use to smell with?' Aadam shakes his head, not understanding. Tai's voice gathers new layers of disgust. 'You know, sir, a thing like an elephant's trunk.' Aziz, seeing what he means, replies: 'A stethoscope? Naturally.' Tai pushes the shikara off from the jetty. Spits. Begins to row away. 'I knew it,' he says. 'You will use such a machine now, instead of your own big nose.'

My grandfather does not trouble to explain that a stethoscope is more like a pair of ears than a nose. He is stifling his own irritation, the resentful anger of a cast-off child; and besides, there is a patient waiting. Time settles down and concentrates on the importance of the moment.

The house was opulent but badly lit. Ghani was a widower and the servants clearly took advantage. There were cobwebs in corners and layers of dust on ledges. They walked down a long corridor; one of the doors was ajar and through it Aziz saw a room in a state of violent disorder. This glimpse, connected with a glint of light in Ghani's dark glasses, suddenly informed Aziz that the landowner was blind. This aggravated his sense of unease: a blind man who claimed to appreciate European paintings? He was, also, impressed, because Ghani hadn't bumped into anything . . . they halted outside a thick teak door. Ghani said, 'Wait here two moments,' and went into the room behind the door.

In later years, Doctor Aadam Aziz swore that during those two moments of solitude in the gloomy spidery corridors of the landowner's mansion he was gripped by an almost uncontrollable desire to turn and run away as fast as his legs would carry him. Unnerved by the enigma of the blind art-lover, his insides filled with tiny scrabbling insects as a result of the insidious venom of Tai's mutterings, his nostrils itching to the point of convincing him that he had somehow contracted venereal disease, he felt his feet begin slowly, as though encased in boots of lead, to turn; felt blood pounding in his temples; and was seized by so powerful a sensation of standing upon a point of no return that he very nearly wet his German woollen trousers. He began, without knowing it, to blush furiously; and at this point his mother appeared before him, seated on the floor before a low desk, a rash spreading like a blush across her face as she held a turquoise up to the light. His mother's face had acquired all the scorn of the boatman Tai. 'Go, go, run,' she told him in Tai's voice, 'Don't worry about your poor old mother.' Doctor Aziz found himself stammering, 'What a useless son you've got, Amma; can't you see there's a hole in the middle of me the size of a melon?' His mother smiled a pained smile. 'You always were a heartless boy,' she sighed, and then turned into a lizard on the wall of the corridor and stuck her tongue out at him. Doctor Aziz stopped feeling dizzy, became unsure that he'd actually spoken aloud, wondered what he'd meant by that business about the hole, found that his feet were no longer trying to escape, and realized that he was being watched. A woman with the biceps of a wrestler was staring at him, beckoning him to follow her into the room. The state of her sari told him that she was a servant; but she was not servile. 'You look green as a fish,' she said. 'You young doctors. You come into a strange house and your liver turns to jelly. Come, Doctor Sahib, they are waiting for you.' Clutching his bag a fraction too tightly, he followed her through the dark teak door.

. . . Into a spacious bedchamber that was as

ill-lit as the rest of the house; although here there were shafts of dusty sunlight seeping in through a fanlight high on one wall. These fusty rays illuminated a scene as remarkable as anything the Doctor had ever witnessed: a tableau of such surpassing strangeness that his feet began to twitch towards the door once again. Two more women, also built like professional wrestlers, stood stiffly in the light, each holding one corner of an enormous white bedsheet, their arms raised high above their heads so that the sheet hung between them like a curtain. Mr Ghani welled up out of the murk surrounding the sunlit sheet and permitted the nonplussed Aadam to stare stupidly at the peculiar tableau for perhaps half a minute, at the end of which, and before a word had been spoken, the Doctor made a discovery:

In the very centre of the sheet, a hole had been cut, a crude circle about seven inches in diameter.

'Close the door, ayah,' Ghani instructed the first of the lady wrestlers, and then, turning to Aziz, became confidential. 'This town contains many good-for-nothings who have on occasion tried to climb into my daughter's room. She needs,' he nodded at the three musclebound women, 'protectors.'

Aziz was still looking at the perforated sheet.

Ghani said, 'All right come on, you will examine my Naseem right now. *Pronto.*'

My grandfather peered around the room. 'But where is she, Ghani Sahib?' he blurted out finally. The lady wrestlers adopted supercilious expressions and, it seemed to him, tightened their musculatures, just in case he intended to try something fancy.

'Ah, I see your confusion,' Ghani said, his poisonous smile broadening 'You Europe-returned chappies forget certain things. Doctor Sahib, my daughter is a decent girl, it goes without saying. She not flaunt her body under the noses of strange men. You understand that you cannot be permitted to see her, no, not in any circumstances; accordingly I have required her to be positioned behind that sheet. She stands there, like a good girl.'

A frantic note had crept into Doctor Aziz's voice. 'Ghani Sahib, tell me how I am to examine her without looking at her?' Ghani smiled on.

'You will kindly specify which portion of my daughter it is necessary to inspect. I will then issue her with my instructions to place the required segment against that hole which you see there. And so, in this fashion the thing may be achieved.'

'But what, in any event, does the lady complain of?' – my grandfather, despairingly. To which Mr Ghani, his eyes rising upwards in their sockets, his smile twisting into a grimace of grief, replied: 'The poor child! She has a terrible, a too dreadful stomach-ache.'

'In that case,' Doctor Aziz said with some restraint, 'will she show me her stomach, please.'

Mercurochrome

Padma – our plump Padma – is sulking magnificently. (She can't read and, like all fish-lovers, dislikes other people knowing anything she doesn't. Padma: strong, jolly, a consolation for my last days. But definitely a bitch-in-the-manger.) She attempts to cajole me from my desk: 'Eat, na, food is spoiling.' I remain stubbornly hunched over paper. 'But what is so precious,' Padma demands, her right hand slicing the air updownup in exasperation, 'to need all this writing-shiting?' I reply: now that I've let out the details of my birth, now that the perforated sheet stands between doctor and patient, there's no going back. Padma snorts. Wrist smacks against forehead. 'Okay, starve starve, who cares two pice?' Another louder, conclusive snort . . . but I take no exception to her attitude. She stirs a bubbling vat all day for a living; something hot and vinegary has steamed her up tonight. Thick of waist, somewhat hairy of forearm, she flounces, gesticulates, exits. Poor Padma. Things are always getting her goat. Perhaps even her name: understandably enough, since her mother told her, when she was only small, that she had been named after the lotus goddess, whose most common appellation amongst village folk is 'The One Who Possesses Dung'.

In the renewed silence, I return to sheets of paper which smell just a little of turmeric, ready and willing to put out of its misery a narrative which I left yesterday hanging in mid-air – just as Scheherazade, depending for her very survival on leaving Prince Shahryar eaten up by curiosity, used to do night after night! I'll begin at once: by revealing that my grandfather's premonitions in the corridor were not without foundation. In the succeeding months and years, he fell under what I can only describe as the sorcerer's spell of that enormous – and as yet unstained – perforated cloth.

'Again?' Aadam's mother said, rolling her eyes. 'I tell you, my child, that girl is so sickly from too much soft living only. Too much sweetmeats and spoiling, because of the absence of a mother's firm hand. But go, take care of your invisible patient, your mother is all right with her little nothing of a headache.'

In those years, you see, the landowner's daughter Naseem Ghani contracted a quite extraordinary number of minor illnesses, and each time a shikara wallah was despatched to summon the tall young

Doctor sahib with the big nose who was making such a reputation for himself in the valley. Aadam Aziz's visits to the bedroom with the shaft of sunlight and the three lady wrestlers became weekly events; and on each occasion he was vouchsafed a glimpse, through the mutilated sheet, of a different seven-inch circle of the young woman's body. Her initial stomach-ache was succeeded by a very slightly twisted right ankle, an ingrowing toenail on the big toe of the left foot, a tiny cut on the lower left calf. ('Tetanus is a killer, Doctor Sahib,' the landowner said, 'My Naseem must not die for a scratch.') There was the matter of her stiff right knee, which the Doctor was obliged to manipulate through the hole in the sheet . . . and after a time the illnesses leapt upwards, avoiding certain unmentionable zones, and began to proliferate around her upper half. She suffered from something mysterious which her father called Finger Rot, which made the skin flake off her hands; from weakness of the wrist-bones, for which Aadam prescribed calcium tablets; and from attacks of constipation, for which he gave her a course of laxatives, since there was no question of being permitted to administer an enema. She had fevers and she also had subnormal temperatures. At these times his thermometer would be placed under her armpit and he would hum and haw about the relative inefficiency of the method. In the opposite armpit she once developed a slight case of tineachloris and he dusted her with yellow powder; after this treatment – which required him to rub the powder in, gently but firmly, although the soft secret body began to shake and quiver and he heard helpless laughter coming through the sheet, because Naseem Ghani was very ticklish – the itching went away, but Naseem soon found a new set of complaints. She waxed anaemic in the summer and bronchial in the winter. ('Her tubes are most delicate,' Ghani explained, 'like little flutes.') Far away the Great War moved from crisis to crisis, while in the cobwebbed house Doctor Aziz was also engaged in a total war against his sectioned patient's inexhaustible complaints. And, in all those war years, Naseem never repeated an illness. 'Which only shows,' Ghani told him, 'that you are a good doctor. When you cure, she is cured for good. But alas!' – he struck his forehead – 'She pines for her late mother, poor baby, and her body suffers. She is a too loving child.'

So gradually Doctor Aziz came to have a picture of Naseem in his mind, a badly-fitting collage of her severally-inspected parts. This phantasm of a partitioned woman began to haunt him, and not only in his dreams. Glued together by his imagination, she accompanied him on all his rounds, she moved into the front room of his mind, so that waking and sleeping he could feel in his fingertips the softness of her ticklish skin or the perfect tiny wrists or the beauty of the ankles; he could smell her scent of lavender and chambeli; he could hear her voice and her helpless laughter of a little girl; but she was headless, because he had never seen her face.

His mother lay on her bed, spreadeagled on her stomach. 'Come, come and press me,' she said, 'my doctor son whose fingers can soothe his old mother's muscles. Press, press, my child with his expression of a constipated goose.' He kneaded her shoulders. She grunted, twitched, relaxed. 'Lower now,' she said, 'now higher. To the right. Good. My brilliant son who cannot see what that Ghani landowner is doing. So clever, my child, but he doesn't guess why that girl is forever ill with her piffling disorders. Listen, my boy: see the nose on your face for once: that Ghani thinks you are a good catch for her. Foreign-educated and all. I have worked in shops and been undressed by the eyes of strangers so that you should marry that Naseem! Of course I am right; otherwise why would he look twice at our family?' Aziz pressed his mother. 'O God, stop now, no need to kill me because I tell you the truth!'

By 1918, Adam Aziz had come to live for his regular trips across the lake. And now his eagerness became even more intense, because it became clear that, after three years, the landowner and his daughter had become willing to lower certain barriers. Now, for the first time, Ghani said, 'A lump in the right chest. Is it worrying, Doctor? Look. Look well.' And there, framed in the hole, was a perfectly-formed and lyrically lovely . . . 'I must touch it,' Aziz said, fighting with his voice. Ghani slapped him on the back. 'Touch, touch!' he cried, 'The hands of the healer! The curing touch, eh, Doctor?' And Aziz reached out a hand . . . 'Forgive me for asking; but is it the lady's time of the month?' . . . Little secret smiles appearing on the faces of the lady wrestlers. Ghani, nodding affably: 'Yes. Don't be so embarrassed, old chap. We are family and doctor now.' And Aziz, 'Then don't worry. The lumps will go when the time ends.' . . . And the next time, 'A pulled muscle in the back of her thigh, Doctor Sahib. Such pain!' And there, in the sheet, weakening the eyes of Aadam Aziz, hung a superbly rounded and impossible buttock . . . And now Aziz: 'Is it permitted that . . .' Whereupon a word from Ghani; an obedient reply from behind the sheet; a drawstring pulled; and pajamas fall from the celestial rump, which swells wondrously through the hole. Aadam Aziz forces himself into a medical frame of mind . . . reaches out . . . feels. And swears to himself, in amazement, that he sees the bottom reddening in a shy, but compliant blush.

That evening, Aadam contemplated the blush. Did the magic of the sheet work on both sides of the hole? Excitedly, he envisaged his headless Naseem tingling beneath the scrutiny of his eyes, his thermometer, his stethoscope, his fingers, and trying to build a picture in her mind of *him*. She was at a disadvantage, of course, having seen nothing but his hands . . . Aadam began to hope with an illicit desperation for Naseem Ghani to develop a migraine or graze her unseen chin, so they could look each other in the face. He knew how unprofessional his feelings were; but did nothing to stifle them. There was not much he could do. They had acquired a life of their own. In short: my grandfather had fallen in love, and had come to think of the perforated sheet as something sacred and magical, because through it he had seen the things which had filled up the hole inside him which had been created when he had been hit on the nose by a tussock and insulted by the boatman Tai.

On the day the World War ended, Naseem developed the longed-for headache. Such historical coincidences have littered, and perhaps befouled, my family's existence in the world.

He hardly dared to look at what was framed in the hole in the sheet. Maybe she was hideous; perhaps that explained all this performance . . . he looked. And saw a soft face that was not at all ugly, a cushioned setting for her glittering, gemstone eyes, which were brown with flecks of gold: tiger's-eyes. Doctor Aziz's fall was complete. And Naseem burst out, 'But Doctor, my God, what a *nose*!' Ghani, angrily, 'Daughter, mind your . . .' But patient and doctor were laughing together, and Aziz was saying, 'Yes, yes, it is a remarkable specimen. They tell me there are dynasties waiting in it . . .' And he bit his tongue because he had been about to add, '. . . like snot.'

And Ghani, who had stood blindly beside the sheet for three long years, smiling and smiling and smiling, began once again to smile his secret smile, which was mirrored in the lips of the wrestlers.

Meanwhile, the boatman, Tai, had taken his unexplained decision to give up washing. In a valley drenched in freshwater lakes, where even the very poorest people could (and did) pride themselves on their cleanliness, Tai chose to stink. For three years now, he had neither bathed nor washed himself after answering calls of nature. He wore the same clothes, unwashed, year in, year out; his one concession to winter was to put his chugha-coat over his putrescent pajamas. The little basket of hot coals which he carried inside the chugha, in the Kashmiri fashion, to keep him warm in the bitter cold, only animated and accentuated his evil odours. He took to drifting slowly past the Aziz household, releasing the dreadful fumes of his body across the small garden and into the house. Flowers died; birds fled from the ledge outside old Father Aziz's window. Naturally, Tai lost work; the English in particular were reluctant to be ferried by a human cesspit. The story went around the lake that Tai's wife, driven to distraction by the old man's sudden filthiness, pleaded for a reason. He had answered: 'Ask our foreign-returned doctor, ask that nakkoo, that German Aziz.' Was it, then, an attempt to offend the Doctor's hypersensitive nostrils (in which the itch of danger had subsided somewhat under the anaesthetizing ministrations of love)? Or a gesture of unchangingness in defiance of the invasion of the doctori-attaché from Heidelberg? Once Aziz asked the ancient, straight out, what it was all for; but Tai only breathed on him and rowed away. The breath nearly felled Aziz; it was sharp as an axe.

In 1918, Doctor Aziz's father, deprived of his

birds, died in his sleep; and at once his mother, who had been able to sell the gemstone business thanks to the success of Aziz's practice, and who now saw her husband's death as a merciful release for her from a life filled with responsibilities, took to her own deathbed and followed her man before the end of his own forty-day mourning period. By the time the Indian regiments returned at the end of the war, Doctor Aziz was an orphan, and a free man – except that his heart had fallen through a hole some seven inches across.

Desolating effect of Tai's behaviour: it ruined Doctor Aziz's good relations with the lake's floating population. He, who as a child had chatted freely with fishwives and flower-sellers, found himself looked at askance. 'Ask that nakkoo, that German Aziz.' Tai had branded him as an alien, and therefore a person not completely to be trusted. They didn't like the boatman, but they found the transformation which the Doctor had evidently worked upon him even more disturbing. Aziz found himself suspected, even ostracized, by the poor; and it hurt him badly. Now he understood what Tai was up to: the man was trying to chase him out of the valley.

The story of the perforated sheet got out, too. The lady wrestlers were evidently less discreet than they looked. Aziz began to notice people pointing at him. Women giggled behind their palms . . .

'I've decided to give Tai his victory,' he said. The three lady wrestlers, two holding up the sheet, the third hovering near the door, strained to hear him through the cotton wool in their ears. ('I made my father do it,' Naseem told him, 'These chatterjees won't do any more of their tittling and tattling from now on.') Naseem's eyes, hole-framed, became wider than ever.

. . . Just like his own when, a few days earlier, he had been walking the city streets, had seen the last bus of the winter arrive, painted with its colourful inscriptions – on the front, GOD WILLING in green shadowed in red; on the back, blue-shadowed yellow crying THANK GOD!, and in cheeky maroon, SORRY-BYE-BYE! – and had recognized, through a web of new rings and lines on her face, Ilse Lubin as she descended . . .

Nowadays, Ghani the landowner left him alone with earplugged guardians, 'To talk a little; the doctor-patient relationship can only deepen in strictest confidentiality. I see that now, Aziz Sahib – forgive my earlier intrusions.' Nowadays, Naseem's tongue was getting freer all the time. 'What kind of talk is this? What are you – a man or a mouse? To leave home because of a stinky shikara-man!' . . .

'Oskar died,' Ilse told him, sipping fresh lime water on his mother's takht. 'Like a comedian. He went to talk to the army and tell them not to be pawns. The fool really thought the troops would fling down their guns and walk away. We watched from a window and I prayed they wouldn't just trample all over him. The regiment had learned to march in step by then, you wouldn't recognize them. As he reached the streetcorner across from the parade ground he tripped over his own shoelace and fell into the street. A staff car hit him and he died. He could never keep his laces tied, that ninny' . . . here there were diamonds freezing in her lashes . . . 'He was the type that gives anarchists a bad name.'

'All right,' Naseem conceded, 'so you've got a good chance of landing a good job. Agra University, it's a famous place, don't think I don't know. University doctor! . . . sounds good. Say you're going for that, and it's a different business.' Eyelashes drooped in the hole. 'I will miss you, naturally . . .'

'I'm in love,' Aadam Aziz said to Ilse Lubin. And later, '. . . So I've only seen her through a hole in a sheet, one part at a time; and I swear her bottom blushes.'

'They must be putting something in the air up here,' Ilse said.

'Naseem, I've got the job,' Aadam said excitedly.

'The letter came today. With effect from April 1919. Your father says he can find a buyer for my house and the gemstone shop also.'

'Wonderful,' Naseem pouted. 'So now I must find a new doctor. Or maybe I'll get that old hag again who didn't know two things about anything.'

'Because I am an orphan,' Doctor Aziz said, 'I must come myself in place of my family members. But I have come nevertheless, Ghani Sahib, for the first time without being sent for. This is not a professional visit.'

'Dear boy!' Ghani, clapping Aadam on the back. 'Of course you must marry her. With an A-1 fine dowry! No expense spared! It will be the wedding of the year, oh most certainly, yes!'

'I cannot leave you behind when I go,' Aziz said to Naseem. Ghani said, 'Enough of this tamasha! No more need for this sheet tomfoolery! Drop it down, you women, these are young lovers now!'

'At last,' said Aadam Aziz, 'I see you whole at last. But I must go now. My rounds . . . and an old friend is staying with me, I must tell her, she will be very happy for us both. A dear friend from Germany.'

'No, Aadam baba,' his bearer said, 'since the morning I have not seen Ilse Begum. She hired that old Tai to go for a shikara ride.'

'What can be said, sir?' Tai mumbled meekly. 'I am honoured indeed to be summoned into the home of a so-great personage as yourself. Sir, the lady hired me for a trip to the Mughal Gardens, to do it before the lake freezes. A quiet lady, Doctor Sahib, not one word out of her all the time. So I was thinking my own unworthy private thoughts as old fools will and suddenly when I look she is not in her seat. Sahib, on my wife's head I swear it, it is not possible to see over the back of the seat, how was I to tell? Believe a poor old boatman who was your friend when you were young . . .'

'Aadam baba,' the old bearer interrupted, 'excuse me but just now I have found this paper on her table.'

'I know where she is,' Doctor Aziz stared at Tai. 'I don't know how you keep getting mixed up in my life; but you showed me the place once. You said: certain foreign women come here to drown.'

'I, Sahib?' Tai shocked, malodorous, innocent. 'But grief is making your head play trick! How can I know these things?'

And after the body, bloated, wrapped in weeds, had been dredged up by a group of blank-faced boatmen, Tai visited the shikara halt and told the men there, as they recoiled from his breath of a bullock with dysentery, 'He blames me, only

imagine! Brings his loose Europeans here and tells
me it is my fault when they jump into the lake! . . .
I ask, how did he know just where to look? Yes, ask
him that, ask that nakkoo Aziz!'

She had left a note. It read: 'I didn't mean it.'

I make no comment; these events, which have
tumbled from my lips any old how, garbled by haste
and emotion, are for others to judge. Let me be
direct now, and say that during the long, hard winter
of 1918–19, Tai fell ill, contracting a violent skin
disease, akin to that European curse called the King's
Evil; but he refused to see Doctor Aziz, and was
treated by a local homeopath. And in March, when
the lake thawed, a marriage took place in a large
marquee in the grounds of Ghani the landowner's
house. The wedding contract assured Aadam Aziz
of a respectable sum of money, which would help
buy a house in Agra, and the dowry included, at
Doctor Aziz's especial request, a certain mutilated
bedsheet. The young couple sat on a dais, garlanded
and cold, while the guests filed past dropping rupees
into their laps. That night my grandfather placed
the perforated sheet beneath his bride and himself
and in the morning it was adorned by three drops
of blood, which formed a small triangle. In the
morning, the sheet was displayed, and after the

consummation ceremony a limousine hired by the landowner arrived to drive my grandparents to Amritsar, where they would catch the Frontier Mail. Mountains crowded round and stared as my grandfather left his home for the last time. (He would return, once, but not to leave.) Aziz thought he saw an ancient boatman standing on land to watch them pass – but it was probably a mistake, since Tai was ill. The blister of a temple atop Sankara Acharya, which Muslims had taken to calling the Takht-e-Sulaiman, or Seat of Solomon, paid them no attention. Winter-bare poplars and snow-covered fields of saffron undulated around them as the car drove south, with an old leather bag containing, amongst other things, a stethoscope and a bedsheet, packed in the boot. Doctor Aziz felt, in the pit of his stomach, a sensation akin to weightlessness.

Or falling.

(. . . And now I am cast as a ghost. I am nine years old and the whole family, my father, my mother, the Brass Monkey and myself, are staying at my grandparents' house in Agra, and the grandchildren – myself among them – are staging the customary New Year's play; and I have been cast as a ghost. Accordingly – and surreptitiously so as to preserve the secrets of the forthcoming theatricals – I am ransacking the house for a spectral disguise.

My grandfather is out and about his rounds. I am in his room. And here on top of this cupboard is an old trunk, covered in dust and spiders, but unlocked. And here, inside it, is the answer to my prayers. Not just a sheet, but one with a hole already cut in it! Here it is, inside this leather bag inside this trunk, right beneath an old stethoscope and a tube of mildewed Vick's Inhaler ... the sheet's appearance in our show was nothing less than a sensation. My grandfather took one look at it and rose roaring to his feet. He strode up on stage and unghosted me right in front of everyone. My grandmother's lips were so tightly pursed they seemed to disappear. Between them, the one booming at me in the voice of a forgotten boatman, the other conveying her fury through vanished lips, they reduced the awesome ghost to a weeping wreck. I fled, took to my heels and ran into the little cornfield, not knowing what had happened. I sat there – perhaps on the very spot on which Nadir Khan had sat! – for several hours, swearing over and over that I would never again open a forbidden trunk, and feeling vaguely resentful that it had not been locked in the first place. But I knew, from their rage, that the sheet was somehow very important indeed.)

I have been interrupted by Padma, who brought me

my dinner and then withheld it, blackmailing me: 'So if you're going to spend all your time wrecking your eyes with that scribbling, at least you must read it to me.' I have been singing for my supper – but perhaps our Padma will be useful, because it's impossible to stop her being a critic. She is particularly angry with my remarks about her name. 'What do you know, city boy?' she cried – hand slicing the air. 'In my village there is no shame in being named for the Dung Goddess. Write at once that you are wrong, completely.' In accordance with my lotus's wishes, I insert, forthwith, a brief paean to Dung.

Dung, that fertilizes and causes the crops to grow! Dung, which is patted into thin chapati-like cakes when still fresh and moist, and is sold to the village builders, who use it to secure and strengthen the walls of kachcha buildings made of mud! Dung, whose arrival from the nether end of cattle goes a long way towards explaining their divine and sacred status! Oh, yes, I was wrong, I admit I was prejudiced, no doubt because its unfortunate odours do have a way of offending my sensitive nose – how wonderful, how ineffably lovely it must be to be named for the Purveyor of Dung!

. . . On April 6th, 1919, the holy city of Amritsar smelled (gloriously, Padma, celestially!) of excrement. And perhaps the (beauteous!) reek did not offend the Nose on my grandfather's face – after all, Kashmiri peasants used it, as described above, for a kind of plaster. Even in Srinagar, hawkers with barrows of round dung-cakes were not an uncommon sight. But then the stuff was drying, muted, useful. Amritsar dung was fresh and (worse) redundant. Nor was it all bovine. It issued from the rumps of the horses between the shafts of the city's many tongas, ikkas and gharries; and mules and men and dogs attended nature's calls, mingling in a brotherhood of shit. But there were cows, too: sacred kine roaming the dusty streets, each patrolling its own territory, staking its claims in excrement. And flies! Public Enemy Number One, buzzing gaily from turd to steaming turd, celebrated and cross-pollinated these freely-given offerings. The city swarmed about, too, mirroring the motion of the flies. Doctor Aziz looked down from his hotel window on to this scene as a Jain in a facemask walked past, brushing the pavement before him with a twig-broom, to avoid stepping on an ant, or even a fly. Spicy sweet fumes rose from a street-snack barrow. 'Hot pakoras, pakoras hot!' A white woman was buying silks from a shop across the street and men in turbans were ogling her. Naseem – now Naseem Aziz – had a sharp headache; it was the first time she'd ever repeated an illness, but life outside her quiet valley had come as something of a shock to her. There was a jug of fresh lime water by her bed, emptying rapidly. Aziz stood at the window, inhaling the city. The spire of the Golden Temple gleamed in the sun. But his nose itched: something was not right here.

Close-up of my grandfather's right hand: nails knuckles fingers all somehow bigger than you'd expect. Clumps of red hair on the outside edges. Thumb and forefinger pressed together, separated only by a thickness of paper. In short: my grandfather was holding a pamphlet. It had been inserted into his hand (we cut to a long-shot – nobody from Bombay should be without a basic film vocabulary) as he entered the hotel foyer. Scurrying of urchin through revolving door, leaflets falling in his wake, as the chaprassi gives chase. Mad revolutions in the doorway, roundandround; until chaprassi-hand demands a close-up, too, because it is pressing thumb to forefinger, the two separated only by the thickness of urchin-ear. Ejection of juvenile disseminator of gutter-tracts; but still my grandfather retained the message. Now, looking out of his window, he sees it echoed on a wall opposite; and there, on the minaret of a mosque; and in the large black type of newsprint under a hawker's arm. Leaflet newspaper mosque and wall are crying:

Hartal! Which is to say, literally speaking, a day of mourning, of stillness, of silence. But this is India in the heyday of the Mahatma, when even language obeys the instructions of Gandhiji, and the word has acquired, under his influence, new resonances. *Hartal – April 7,* agree mosque newspaper wall and pamphlet, because Gandhi has decreed that the whole of India shall, on that day, come to a halt. To mourn, in peace, the continuing presence of the British.

'I do not understand this hartal when nobody is dead,' Naseem is crying softly. 'Why will the train not run? How long are we stuck for?'

Doctor Aziz notices a soldierly young man in the street, and thinks – the Indians have fought for the British; so many of them have seen the world by now, and been tainted by Abroad. They will not easily go back to the old world. The British are wrong to try and turn back the clock. 'It was a mistake to pass the Rowlatt Act,' he murmurs.

'What rowlatt?' wails Naseem. 'This is nonsense where I'm concerned!'

'Against political agitation,' Aziz explains, and returns to his thoughts. Tai once said: 'Kashmiris are different. Cowards, for instance. Put a gun in a Kashmiri's hand and it will have to go off by itself – he'll never dare to pull the trigger. We are not like

Indians, always making battles.' Aziz, with Tai in his head, does not feel Indian. Kashmir, after all, is not strictly speaking a part of the Empire, but an independent princely state. He is not sure if the hartal of pamphlet mosque wall newspaper is his fight, even though he is in occupied territory now. He turns from the window . . .

. . . To see Naseem weeping into a pillow. She has been weeping ever since he asked her, on their second night, to move a little. 'Move where?' she asked. 'Move how?' He became awkward and said, 'Only move, I mean, like a woman . . .' She shrieked in horror. 'My God, what have I married? I know you Europe-returned men. You find terrible women and then you try to make us girls be like them! Listen, Doctor Sahib, husband or no husband, I am not any . . . bad word woman.' This was a battle my grandfather never won; and it set the tone for their marriage, which rapidly developed into a place of frequent and devastating warfare, under whose depredations the young girl behind the sheet and the gauche young Doctor turned rapidly into different, stranger beings . . . 'What now, wife?' Aziz asks. Naseem buries her face in the pillow. 'What else?' she says in muffled tones. 'You, or what? You want me to walk naked in front of strange men.' (He has told her to come out of purdah.)

He says, 'Your shirt covers you from neck to wrist to knee. Your loose pajamas hide you down to and including your ankles. What we have left are your feet and face. Wife, are your face and feet obscene?' But she wails, 'They will see more than that! They will see my deep-deep shame!'

And now an accident, which launches us into the world of Mercurochrome . . . Aziz, finding his temper slipping from him, drags all his wife's purdah-veils from her suitcase, flings them into a wastepaper basket made of tin with a painting of Guru Nanak on the side, and sets fire to them. Flames leap up, taking him by surprise, licking at curtains. Aadam rushes to the door and yells for help as the cheap curtains begin to blaze . . . and bearers guests washerwomen stream into the room and flap at the burning fabric with dusters towels and other people's laundry. Buckets are brought; the fire goes out; and Naseem cowers on the bed as about thirty-five Sikhs, Hindus and untouchables throng in the smoke-filled room. Finally they leave, and Naseem unleashes two sentences before clamping her lips obstinately shut.

'You are a mad man. I want more lime water.'

My grandfather opens the windows, turns to his bride. 'The smoke will take time to go; I will take a walk. Are you coming?'

Lips clamped; eyes squeezed; a single violent No from the head; and my grandfather goes into the streets alone. His parting shot: 'Forget about being a good Kashmiri girl. Start thinking about being a modern Indian woman.'

. . . While in the Cantonment area, at British Army H.Q., one Brigadier R. E. Dyer is waxing his moustache.

It is April 7th, 1919, and in Amritsar the Mahatma's grand design is being distorted. The shops have shut; the railway station is closed; but now rioting mobs are breaking them up. Doctor Aziz, leather bag in hand, is out in the streets, giving help wherever possible. Trampled bodies have been left where they fell. He is bandaging wounds, daubing them liberally with Mercurochrome, which makes them look bloodier than ever, but at least disinfects them. Finally he returns to his hotel room, his clothes soaked in red stains, and Naseem commences a panic. 'Let me help, let me help, Allah what a man I've married, who goes into gullies to fight with goondas!' She is all over him with water on wads of cotton wool. 'I don't know why can't you be a respectable doctor like ordinary people are just cure important illnesses and all? O God you've got blood everywhere! Sit, sit now, let me wash you at least!'

'It isn't blood, wife.'

'You think I can't see for myself with my own eyes? Why must you make a fool of me even when you're hurt? Must your wife not look after you, even?'

'It's Mercurochrome, Naseem. Red medicine.'

Naseem – who had become a whirlwind of activity, seizing clothes, running taps – freezes. 'You do it on purpose,' she says, 'to make me look stupid. I am not stupid. I have read several books.'

It is April 13th, and they are still in Amritsar. 'This affair isn't finished,' Aadam Aziz told Naseem. 'We can't go, you see: they may need doctors again.'

'So we must sit here and wait until the end of the world?'

He rubbed his nose. 'No, not so long, I am afraid.'

That afternoon, the streets are suddenly full of people, all moving in the same direction, defying Dyer's new Martial Law regulations. Aadam tells Naseem, 'There must be a meeting planned – there will be trouble from the military. They have banned meetings.'

'Why do you have to go? Why not wait to be called?'

... A compound can be anything from a waste-land to a park. The largest compound in Amritsar

59

is called Jallianwala Bagh. It is not grassy. Stones cans glass and other things are everywhere. To get into it, you must walk down a very narrow alleyway between two buildings. On April 13th, many thousands of Indians are crowding through this alleyway. 'It is peaceful protest,' someone tells Doctor Aziz. Swept along by the crowds, he arrives at the mouth of the alley. A bag from Heidelberg is in his right hand. (No close-up is necessary.) He is, I know, feeling very scared, because his nose is itching worse than it ever has; but he is a trained doctor, he puts it out of his mind, he enters the compound. Somebody is making a passionate speech. Hawkers move through the crowd selling channa and sweet-meats. The air is filled with dust. There do not seem to be any goondas, any troublemakers, as far as my grandfather can see. A group of Sikhs has spread a cloth on the ground and is eating, seated around it. There is still a smell of ordure in the air. Aziz penetrates the heart of the crowd, as Brigadier R. E. Dyer arrives at the entrance to the alleyway, followed by fifty crack troops. He is the Martial Law Commander of Amritsar – an important man, after all; the waxed tips of his moustache are rigid with importance. As the fifty-one men march down the alleyway a tickle replaces the itch in my grandfather's nose. The fifty-one men enter the compound and take up positions, twenty-five to Dyer's right and twenty-five to his left; and Aadam Aziz ceases to concentrate on the events around him as the tickle mounts to unbearable intensities. As Brigadier Dyer issues a command the sneeze hits my grandfather full in the face. 'Yaaaakh-*thooo!*' he sneezes and falls forward, losing his balance, following his nose and thereby saving his life. His 'doctori-attaché' flies open; bottles, liniment and syringes scatter in the dust. He is scrabbling furiously at people's feet, trying to save his equipment before it is crushed. There is a noise like teeth chattering in winter and someone falls on him. Red stuff stains his shirt. There are screams now and sobs and the strange chattering continues. More and more people seem to have stumbled and fallen on top of my grandfather. He becomes afraid for his back. The clasp of his bag is digging into his chest, inflicting upon it a bruise so severe and mysterious that it will not fade until after his death, years later, on the hill of Sankara Acharya or Takht-e-Sulaiman. His nose is jammed against a bottle of red pills. The chattering stops and is replaced by the noises of people and birds. There seems to be no traffic noise whatsoever. Brigadier Dyer's fifty men put down their machine-guns and go away. They have fired a total of one thousand six hundred and fifty rounds into the unarmed crowd. Of these, one thousand five hundred and sixteen have found their mark, killing or wounding some person. 'Good shooting,' Dyer tells his men, 'We have done a jolly good thing.'

When my grandfather got home that night, my grandmother was trying hard to be a modern woman, to please him, and so she did not turn a hair at his appearance. 'I see you've been spilling the Mercurochrome again, clumsy,' she said, appeasingly.

'It's blood,' he replied, and she fainted. When he brought her round with the help of a little sal volatile, she said, 'Are you hurt?'

'No,' he said.

'But *where* have you *been*, my *God*?'

'Nowhere on earth,' he said, and began to shake in her arms.

My own hand, I confess, has begun to wobble; not entirely because of its theme, but because I have noticed a thin crack, like a hair, appearing in my wrist, beneath the skin . . . No matter. We all owe death a life. So let me conclude with the uncorroborated rumour that the boatman Tai, who recovered from his scrofulous infection soon after my grandfather left Kashmir, did not die until 1947, when (the story goes) he was infuriated by India and Pakistan's struggle over his valley, and walked to Chhamb with the express purpose of standing between the opposing forces and giving them a piece of his mind. Kashmiri for the Kashmiris: that was his line. Naturally, they shot him. Oskar Lubin would probably have approved of his rhetorical gesture; R. E. Dyer might have commended his murderers' rifle skills

I must go to bed. Padma is waiting; and I need a little warmth.